CASE FILES

UNS LVED

THE CHASE

Edited By Wendy Laws

First published in Great Britain in 2023 by:

Young Writers
Remus House
Coltsfoot Drive
Peterborough
PE2 9BF
Telephone: 01733 890066
Website: www.youngwriters.co.uk

Printed and bound in the UK by BookPrintingUK
Website: www.bookprintinguk.com
YB0566G

FOREWORD

As long as there have been people, there has been crime, and as long as there have been people, there have also been stories. Crime fiction has a long history and remains a consistent best-seller to this day. It was for this reason that we decided to delve into the murky underworld of criminals and their misdeeds for our newest writing competition.

We challenged secondary school students to craft a story in just 100 words on the theme of 'Unsolved'. They were encouraged to consider all elements of crime and mystery stories: the crime itself, the victim, the suspect, the investigators, the judge and jury. The result is a variety of styles and narrations, from the smallest misdemeanors to the most heinous of crimes. Will the victims get justice or will the suspects get away with murder? There's only one way to find out!

Here at Young Writers it's our aim to inspire the next generation and instill in them a love of creative writing, and what better way than to see their work in print? The imagination and flair on show in these stories is proof that we might just be achieving that aim! The characters within these pages may have to prove their innocence, but these authors have already proved their skill at writing!

CONTENTS

Macy Loxley (15)	58	Brody Ballard (12)	101
Krystal Gunner (12)	59	Abigail Parks (12)	102
Ellie Lewis (11)	60	Oliver Key (12)	103
Evie Richardson (13)	61	Bianca Preda (14)	104
Chester Green (12)	62	Matthew Achanso Tamanji (12)	105
Cameron Wade (15)	63	Jayden Wilmer (14)	106
Lily Esberger (11)	64		
Oliver Lacey (13)	65		

Macy Loxley (15) — 58
Krystal Gunner (12) — 59
Ellie Lewis (11) — 60
Evie Richardson (13) — 61
Chester Green (12) — 62
Cameron Wade (15) — 63
Lily Esberger (11) — 64
Oliver Lacey (13) — 65
Mason Cordell (12) — 66
Grace Clipsham (14) — 67
Josh Myhill (13) — 68
Abigail Clarke (13) — 69
Shyla Stewart (12) — 70
Lucy Matchett (13) — 71
Mohamed Bridan (12) — 72
Willow Reid (12) — 73
Viktoria Jakovleva (15) — 74
Chelsey Newton (12) — 75
Summer Lloyd (14) — 76
Jack Johnson (12) — 77
Adam Blaszkiewicz (12) — 78
Jesse Osaje (12) — 79
Erin Mallard (12) — 80
Riley Langridge (13) — 81
Ashton Gillyett (15) — 82
Ruari Sheeran (13) — 83
Emily Cierpka (12) — 84
Kacie Clarke (12) — 85
Kian Robinson (12) — 86
Isabelle Keating (12) — 87
Alfie Middlebrook (12) — 88
Chloe Delaney (11) — 89
Callum Purkis (12) — 90
Leo Sawyer (12) — 91
Ollie Smith (12) — 92
Bethany Hewson (14) — 93
Lily-Mae Fearon (12) — 94
Lani Johnson (11) — 95
Penny Hatton (12) — 96
Jack Cartwright (12) — 97
Cody Durrance (12) — 98
Kyla Cassell (13) — 99
Matas Ulkstinas (13) — 100

Brody Ballard (12) — 101
Abigail Parks (12) — 102
Oliver Key (12) — 103
Bianca Preda (14) — 104
Matthew Achanso Tamanji (12) — 105
Jayden Wilmer (14) — 106

Littleover Community School, Littleover

Aayan Malik (15) — 107
Vanessa Lezama (12) — 108
Shereen Aslam (15) — 109
Haniyah Shakeb (12) — 110
Abdur-Rahman Imran — 111
Joseph Law (13) — 112
Alishah Raja (14) — 113
Holly Gibbon (14) — 114

Pentrehafod School, Hafod

Archie Davidson (13) — 115
Eva Young (11) — 116
Owain Phillips (12) — 117
Isabelle Whitefoot (13) — 118
Jacob T Lewis (12) — 119
Charnia Wilshese-Butler (12) — 120

Pyrland School, Taunton

Alexander Wood (14) — 121
Keiran Prince (13) — 122
Ella Duheaume (13) — 123

St Gregory's Catholic College, Odd Down

Florence Haines (12) — 124
Veritas Okokhere (13) — 125
Ayla Rowland (12) — 126
Tilly While (13) — 127

St John Fisher Catholic Voluntary Academy, Dewsbury

Michal Chodurski (13)	128
Safa Hussain (13)	129
Annie Dean (13)	130
Caylass Toohey (13)	131

St Paul's Catholic College, Burgess Hill

Sophia Hermoso (13)	132
Aleena Joseph (13)	133
Shreya Paul (13)	134

Ysgol John Bright, Llandudno

Dylan Johnson-Middlehurst (12)	135
Alana Owen (12)	136
Holly Pitts (12)	137
Levi Gravett (12)	138
Nosakhare Enaruna (12)	139
Maisie Brown (12)	140
Julia Lament (12)	141

THE STORIES

She's In Her Grave - Now She's Not

I walked into the graveyard, expecting to find my wife, Tara 'sleeping' in her grave. I was happy even if she was dead, I would still be able to 'feel' her presence but as I walked over to her grave, I saw police officers. They were standing at her tombstone. "What's going on?" I said.
"Your wife, Sir," they said. "She's gone!"
"What? Don't be ridiculous! My wife's dead!"
"See for yourself," they said.
As I looked at my wife's grave, all I saw was a bottomless pit. Someone or 'something' must have taken her corpse. The question was; who?

Margi Gungui-Moro (16)
Centre Academy London, Battersea

A Bribe

Michael opened the door to behold a middle-aged man, sitting at a desk, emersed in his typewriter. Without even looking at him, the man snapped, "What do you want?" Michael smirked, taking his cigar out of his mouth. "Say you like money?"
The police chief finally turned to him. "Who the hell are you?"
Michael slowly walked balefully towards him. "I'm just a guy who wants to do business with another."
The office interrupted, "I don't take bribes." Now his eyes were on the typewriter again, his interest in Michael lost, who in turn slowly unclad his smile.

Michele De Gregorio (13)
Centre Academy London, Battersea

The Scarlet Thread

Murder. Poison. Mystery. The words are elegant, poised. They evoke thoughts of fine clothes and high-society parties. The reality is less so, the opposite even. Example; the room I find myself in. It would have been nice before, cosy even. The plump armchair, the tall bookshelf, the heavy desk and tasteful decor. They're all overshadowed though, by the crime scene. The body. The blood. Cause of death? Poison. That much is obvious from the body. No mystery there. No, the mystery lies elsewhere, the blood, that word. It appears I'm chasing the scarlet thread of murder. Again. Wait a minute...

Elodie Wells (12)
Churnet View Middle School, Leek

Missing!

This morning I woke up. I made my sister and me some breakfast. My mum said, "Good morning." I said it back. "Please can you walk your sister home tonight," asked Mum. "Aww, Mum, I wanted to go to my friends," I said.
"Sarah, do you think you can walk on your own?" said Mum. "Yes, Mum," said Sarah.
The end of the day bell rang. I saw Lilly. I went to her and went to her house. When I had finished playing I started to walk home. I heard police cars. "It's all my fault!" Sarah had gone missing...

Maisie Morris (12)

Churnet View Middle School, Leek

The Faceless Figure

The night was creeping in and my friends and I were still in the woods unaware of what horror was about to occur. One of my friends, who was collecting rocks saw something strange. "Hey, come over here," he said. "What's that on the rock?" None of us knew, but the answer became clear to us when we saw a trail of the same red substance. It was blood. Darkness fell. We heard howling amongst the trees. Suddenly, one by one, my friends were taken by something sinister. One of them said, "Why doesn't he have a face?"

Alfie Ferns (11)
Churnet View Middle School, Leek

The Shot

Day nine of hunting for the bounty. It's been hard in the desert, but I am resting in an old railway village. I will find him! In the morning, I went to the saloon for a drink, but I found out that they only sold warm, bitter rum, so I disembarked. Suddenly, five men, all armed with AK14s approached, it was him! I couldn't back out of this one, so I reached for my pistol, but I only had a mere two bullets! *Bang!* I was bleeding, I couldn't move! All five of them had shot me! Darkness has come...

Oscar Thomson (12)
Churnet View Middle School, Leek

The Unsolved Case

There was once a case that was never solved. One day, someone was found dead, but all that was found was a head. Nobody was found guilty, but I knew someone did it. Three suspects, but none were found guilty. I'd found some clues and decided to follow them. I saw a shadow; could it be the villain? I followed, but... they were gone. Could this mean someone is still out there, never to be seen? Who knows? Maybe one day they will be caught. I told someone, but they didn't believe me. What happens now...

Ruby Andrews (11)

Churnet View Middle School, Leek

The Tower

My heart's beating fast. I trail my sweaty hand across the crooked stone wall. Why did I listen to Maggie? Why did I say I was brave? I'm not. I'm not! Surely her story's not true but why do I find myself believing her? These steps will never end! What really is at the top of the tower behind that crooked door? No one comes back out. No. It must be made up or is it? Will I live to tell? I finally reach the door, old and broken, not a sound. "Okay, let's open it. 3... 2... 1..."

Caitlin Campbell (12)
Churnet View Middle School, Leek

Guilty

"Guilty." What for you may ask? Well, let me take you to the beginning. It was an ordinary day and there were two girls sitting there and they were giving out food. But when one of the people received the food, he started choking, then when everyone knew about it they called the police and ambulance but it was too late... They were dead! Everyone knew that it was one of the girls but no one knew which one did it...

Abigail Blaymires (12)
Churnet View Middle School, Leek

The Case Of Jonathan Walters

Jonathan Walters was a man who was in and out of prison for homicide but has never really been put away for long because there has never been enough evidence but the police are getting a lot closer to cracking the case. He has killed people in all sorts of ways, even things you didn't think people could do. He is not well known because he has multiple names. He has been on the run for many years.

Jamie Carr (13)
Churnet View Middle School, Leek

The Unsolved Jail Sentence

"Guilty," the judge said slamming his hammer on the table.
"Guilty!" I exclaimed. "I'm not guilty because I didn't do anything," I said angrily.
The police came and took me to jail but I didn't do it. People were still not sure if it was right for me to get sent to jail. Even to this day, my case is still unsolved.

Libbie Ottolini (13)
Churnet View Middle School, Leek

999

The woman was trembling as she dialled 999. The operator said, "Please stay on the line."
When questions were asked she shook her head. "It's my husband you see - I've found him dead."
"Stay with him, help's on the way."
But while being questioned, she couldn't say... Was there a break-in? Had the man taken his life?
The wife began sobbing... nothing seemed to fit. "I promise you it wasn't me... I never did this crime."
She let out a deafening scream, pointing to the back door ajar. "Miss, we need to take a statement. Please get in the police car..."

Hollie Williams (15)
Colmers School, Rednal

Dead

"Dead!" The word echoed out. Silence ringing all around. Chaos broke out.

"What do you mean dead? How? Why?"

"I'm sorry, there isn't much more I can tell you at the moment."

The woman threw herself at the officer. "My daughter isn't dead! She isn't!"

Shrugging her off, the officer stepped back. The officer pushed her back into a chair, a look of confusion spread across his face. "Are you okay?"

"Of course I'm not okay, my daughter is dead!"

The officer took another step back. "Your daughter has been dead for years..."

Imogen Turner (15)

Frome College, Frome

Fixing An Unjust Court Ruling

"Not guilty!" the judge called.

The murderer smirked in my direction, knowing that he was free, knowing that I'd hate this outcome. The victim's family were frozen in shock, in complete disbelief, as their child's murderer was declared innocent. The defence were pleased that they'd 'won'.

And me, the sole witness, the one who brought this case to light, frozen. Not in shock, but in anger. Though I'd predicted this outcome. Luckily, no one had checked my pockets.

My hand didn't shake nor hesitate as I lifted the stolen gun, flicked off the safety, aimed, fired, and hit my target.

Cloe Manaia (16)

Frome College, Frome

The Underworld

Once upon a time, in a small mysterious town, a string of unsolved disappearances haunted the local people. People went missing without a trace, leaving loved ones worried and devastated.

The authorities were baffled, unable to find clues or make sense of the enigma. Rumours spread, connecting the disappearances to an ancient curse that hung over the town.

As fear gripped the community, a curious young woman named Phoebe dived into this darkness, determined to uncover the truth. Her search uncovered a hidden underworld, where a sinister figure lurked. With her courage and tenacity, Phoebe went further into the darkness.

Freddie Corp (15)
Frome College, Frome

The Secret Diary

It was the mystery that had haunted the small town for years. The disappearance of the beloved librarian, Mrs Jenkins, had left the community in shock and disbelief. Despite numerous investigations and searches, her whereabouts remained unsolved. Every year, on the anniversary of her disappearance, the townspeople would gather at the library to light candles and remember her. But as time passed, the memories of Mrs Jenkins began to fade and the case became another unsolved mystery. That was until a young girl stumbled upon an old diary in the library's basement, revealing secrets that could finally solve the case.

Curtis Taylor (15)
Frome College, Frome

Oil

The void smile swung around to face her. Oily, black, dripping skin stretched too tight. Warbling laughter-like chatter crawled up from its throat and rattled the exposed ribs. She ran, through rain, blood pounding, heart racing, until she reached the door. Darting behind and slamming it shut, she stood pressed against the frigid metal, waiting with held breath as the rattling, warbling laughter faded. Her breath released. *Drip... drip... drip...* Cold water slid down her neck, the rain was getting in. She wiped it off slowly. It's wrong. It's slick. A rattle of ribs and the void smile calls.

Tara Whitelaw (15)
Frome College, Frome

A Simple Break-In

"You will be safe," the detective confirmed to the frail witness.

Just a simple break-in. But the simple break-in soon turned into a cold homicide, leaving the victim dead on her bathroom floor.

"You said she was safe!" her husband yelled, thrashing about the precinct in a boiling rage. The officers had to lead him out.

"How could I have missed such a thing?" the detective pondered before stepping out of the room, leaving me more time to cover the unseen evidence. No one alive was going to know it was me who killed her, the detective's assistant.

Esmee Morrison (14)
Frome College, Frome

Hours, Minutes, Seconds

The usual clanking of metal filled the air. Prison guards entered, the already small room becoming claustrophobic as I was escorted toward execution.

Sat on the freezing chair, strapped with even colder leather, they were light yet still the heaviest thing I ever felt. Nobody was there to witness my last breath, except a news reporter and some officials. The room was dimly lit and smelt of pure chemicals combined with metals.

It became hard to breathe as the black bag was placed over my head. I had accepted my fate - framed for another man's sins. I held my breath.

Lakisha Keegan (15)
Frome College, Frome

Karma

Nobody suspected me. I mean, who would? No one ever suspected the victim. It's easy really, if it happened to you, you can't be guilty, right? You can't steal your own identity, right?

Well, the list of suspects went on and on but none were guilty. I knew that. I got a sweet satisfaction in hiding that fact. "It wasn't me, I swear. I promise! I swear on my life, I didn't do it."

Their screams, their cries... I'd almost feel pity, almost. You see, I would if they weren't the world's worst. I mean, it was their deserved karma.

Toni Brooks (14)
Frome College, Frome

In The Briefcase

He stood there, eyes gleaming menacingly in the moonlit sky, his breath hanging like mist in the air. The man reached into his pocket as a limousine pulled up, loud music blasting through the bulletproof glass.

The music stopped and a figure dressed in a dark suit exited the car, drawing a pistol. "Are you alone?" he asked.

"Of course. I assume you have the goods?"

The man in the suit disappeared into the car and emerged holding an iron briefcase with three locks, which he then opened, revealing the thing that would end the world.

Alex Murguiulday (14)
Frome College, Frome

The Mountain

The cold closed in as Darryl trekked through the mountains. These mountains ran just as cold and lonely as 200 years ago. The blood was failing to warm his body, blue covered his skin and his head began to ache.

The avalanche happened two hours ago. Snow still reached the top of each tree. Darryl was balanced atop a tall tree. His inhales became weaker with time until the branch snapped.

He fell and tumbled past branches as his weak body broke the snow. Then he reached the base, bones broken, heart stopped. The man's corpse began to freeze.

Zach Woodward (15)
Frome College, Frome

No Regret

He was a horrible person, that's why I did it. I was helping purify the world from his greedy hands and I don't regret anything. Taking his life is an accomplishment, if anything. A goal that crossed anyone's mind if they were unlucky enough to be acquainted with him.

He had it coming, acting like that. As if he was born with no heart, or feelings for that matter. Anyway, none of that is anyone's problem anymore. The last problem he'll ever cause is how I dispose of his body. I'll make sure no one remembers, but who to frame?

Mia Sant (14)
Frome College, Frome

Room 19

There was a secret in room 19. A great evil that, if unleashed, would destroy everything good in our world. One night, in the rain, Greg was taking his dog, Rex, for a walk in the forest. They needed somewhere to shelter. That was when they came across the old Harrington Hotel, used as a hunting lodge resort decades ago.

They came into the hall and they heard a strange noise coming from room 19. When they went up to investigate, an ominous, red, blinding light was streaming under the door. When they went over to open it, they discovered...

Kaden Mounty (15)
Frome College, Frome

Innocence

Guilty. The word that changed my life. Everyone around me was cheering, excited about my downfall. My lawyer looked at me and whispered, "It's going to be okay."
The five words I had been told most during the trial. But it wasn't. I was going to death row for a murder I didn't commit. Before I even had time to process what happened, I had already been taken and put in handcuffs.
As I walked out of the courtroom, I turned back, looking at my family crying, sobbing. What were they thinking? Did they know I was innocent?

Ellie Cheeseman (15)
Frome College, Frome

I Have More Time Than Money

They say time is money. I was with my loved ones, seven miles from the summit of this mercifully miraculous journey. The cold when we were close to the peak made me shiver like I was touching cold metal, and all my life was pulled and sucked into it. My family were protected, so no cold could get to them.

Seven men waited for me at the top. They looked far away, yet I reached them sooner than predicted. They seemed like ordinary travellers with their hiking sticks and cold-resistant uniforms. The walk down was ahead, the peak behind.

Jack Eyres (15)
Frome College, Frome

Kai In A Pie

There once was a guy and his name was Kai. One day, Kai was talking in the park when he was suddenly feeling mischievous, so he bought a giant pie factory.

The factory was huge and he felt unstoppable. He produced pies left and right, just for himself to eat. Then he felt even more mischievous and created the world's biggest pie! But while creating the world's biggest blueberry pie, he accidentally fell into the pie and no one noticed. He was then baked into it and eaten by the town. No one knew that Kai was in the pie.

Finn Incledon (14)

Frome College, Frome

Guilty

"Guilty!" the judge screamed over a courtroom of people. Gasps filled the air as if the word sucked all the oxygen out of the room.

The tips of my mouth started to curve. I smiled back at the judge, eyes glistening. The sentence was a prize I had won, something I would treasure always. I laughed as all eyes were on me, the joy overwhelming my body, leaking out of me as I cried with joy.

They grabbed me. I turned and smiled brightly at them all. They were quiet, watching me. All you could hear was my echoing laughter.

Evie Millbank (14)

Frome College, Frome

The Chunk Of Flesh

I saw a patch of red on the pavement, accompanied by a small, fleshy lump. I picked it up to find out it was a tattooed piece of skin that had been ripped from someone's body. It looked like a gang tattoo, an odd but symbolic mark, never to come off his skin. The tissue seemed as if it had been washed before being placed in a puddle of purposefully spilt blood, that was now trickling off the pavement and down the drain.
I dropped the skin chunk back to the bloody pavement. Strange, I didn't remember leaving it there.

Millie Heitkamp (14)
Frome College, Frome

The Dead

People say the dead can't talk, but I can hear them all the
time. Every day, constantly gossiping, mumbling, shouting,
crying. It never stops. I may be the only person in the world
that can hear the dead but all this time, I've ignored it.
I've tried everything to get it to stop, but nothing works.
Sometimes, I think I'm crazy, just making it up in my head.
Just once, I'll reply, I thought. Now I do it all the time. I
always do what they tell me to do. When they tell me to join
them, I do it.

Orla Rogers (14)
Frome College, Frome

Guilty

Guilty. Me? Guilty of what? I haven't done anything, but they think that I murdered my sister. My own sister! My own sibling. Why do people need to blame others because they have no clue who actually did it?

I look around the room at all the people looking at me like I'm a monster. One of the policemen knows I didn't do it. He looks at me and says, "Don't worry, you will get out of this mess."

Who would do this? I have been set up. I think I know who did - it was my horrible, spiteful mother.

Kacey Ford (14)
Frome College, Frome

The Missing Cuppa

"I only put it down for two minutes. I only took my eyes off it for thirty seconds. It was gone! Just like that, it was gone! One-third milk, English tea. It vanished. Thing is, Officer, I live alone. Well, with my cat, but that's it. Maybe it was a ghost?"

"Sir, ghosts are not real and here at the station, we have more problems to solve than a missing cuppa. Please go home."

"Wait, the tea... it's behind you."

"What? No, don't be silly. Who put that there?"

Zofia Seccombe (15)
Frome College, Frome

The Basement

Tick-tock! Tick-tock! This was the fourth night Ava couldn't sleep. A strange, eerie, ominous noise was creeping through the floorboards from the basement. Each sleepless night, the noise got louder and the nerves got stronger.

She gave up. She went down to investigate. As she approached the door, an unsettling feeling filled her stomach. She reached for the doorknob and turned it open. *Bang!*

The next morning, her bedroom was empty. The basement door was open and Ava was nowhere to be seen.

Eva Hill (15)

Frome College, Frome

37 Years

The man sat in his cell. 37 long years he had been sat in there - until today. He was on death row.
The family gathered at the window, already in tears. The prisoner was strapped in the chair. He had accepted his fate. The electrocutioner entered the room, a sinister smile on his face. The guy must have been crazy to do this job by choice.
The inmate smiled at his family, trying to show acceptance, but his eyes were sad. With a sigh, he closed his eyes and looked to space. The button was pushed. He was gone.

Maisie Mcdonald (15)
Frome College, Frome

Salem

Beauty is in the eye of the beholder. And I find a certain beauty in death. A single breath of wind grasps at my neck as I remain bound to my sins, the twine scratching my sunkissed skin, bare, vulnerable and exposed to the world as the church determines all our fate. My innocence is a weak defence, tied alone to the stake. A wick burning, the dead angel licking at my heels. It's searing, but pain feels welcome, like an old friend torn from comfort, slicing you inside out. After all, to be a witch is to be free.

Caiden Perkin (15)
Frome College, Frome

1990

Circa 1990, my mother was murdered. It was my birthday; my father had left to collect the cake. My mother and I had been playing Cluedo.

I liked trying to solve the mysteries.

I don't remember much of the incident, although I can picture the lights, the noise of the sirens, the blood. Soon after, my father was arrested on suspicion of murder. He didn't complain or cry, he wasn't like that.

I was asked to testify in court. I didn't. I started seeing a therapist.

It didn't help.

Jasper Carthew (14)
Frome College, Frome

One Minute

One minute, she was there. The next minute, she wasn't. None of us knew what she died of or if she was murdered. We thought she was murdered but the police didn't manage to solve the case. They were on the case for ages and didn't solve it.

I went away to get something and as I walked away, I heard a scream. So I ran back and there she was, on the floor. So I guessed it was murder and she screamed, or she saw something and screamed then died. I didn't know. Neither did the police.

Lucas Chariten (15)
Frome College, Frome

Shooter

Bang! A gun was fired. The bullet came flying out toward a shopkeeper at the back of his shop. I witnessed it through the open doors.

We kept eye contact for a few seconds and then he ran down the dark, murky alley. I followed close behind and saw him on his phone. I climbed up above him to get a good look at his phone. He called 999 and said he had just witnessed a shooter kill a shopkeeper.

He was framing me! I had hate in my heart for this man. I knew what was coming.

Jacob Elkins (14)
Frome College, Frome

The Echoes

In a dimly lit alley, Detective Bjorson surveyed the crime scene. Blood stained the pavement, a silent witness to the savagery that had unfolded. The victim, a wealthy businessman, lay lifeless, a single bullet piercing his heart. Clues were scarce, but Bjorson's gut told him this was no random act. As he delved deeper, a web of deficit unravelled. A business partner's jealousy, a lover's betrayal and a hidden fortune became intertwined. Bjorson's relentless pursuit of truth exposed a deadly conspiracy, leading to a high-stakes showdown.
In the end, justice prevailed, but the echoes of the crime stayed there.

Archie Savage (12)
Lincoln Castle Academy, Lincoln

Falcon

Down in the dark, sirens in the night. They hadn't caught me yet I did not regret it. They deserved this. I read the jar's label 'Digitalis Purpurea'. I winced when I heard the officer say the word 'foxglove'. Frustrated I returned home. I gorged myself on 'steak' and 'lamb'. I wasn't used to the cuisine of the humans. I stood there in pitch-blackness, feathers rustling, guilt worsening. I heard gunshots. I flew but they weren't after me. They carried out a dead child covered in bloodstains but with no visible wounds. More gunshots, blackness, screams, feathers.

Florence Hope-Johnson (12)
Lincoln Castle Academy, Lincoln

Doppelganger

Monday 12th November 2003, a tragic crime scene, leaving two people murdered and the criminal nowhere to be seen. 12:15. "Hello, I'm at Leicester Road. A bank has been broken into, leaving two people potentially unconscious. Please, come quick, please!"

There were two witnesses. Two males who were across the road from the incident. They described the suspect as a white male, bald, around six foot with blue jeans, a blue jumper and black Gazelles.

The mystery is the same description was seen at the restaurant 'The Taste' at the same time as the incident occurred.

Leah Clark (14)
Lincoln Castle Academy, Lincoln

Murder For Money

It just didn't add up, they both knew I didn't do it. "Who?" The so-called detective demanded from me. "Just one name and you're free to go." He glared at me.
"Act as if you're clueless," the words haunted the back of my head. "Just don't make me a suspect," she commanded.
"If you know I didn't do it, then let me go, you know I'm not capable of doing such a crime." I lost eye contact with him.
"Look, I'll make sure they're gone."
"I'm getting that money any way I can."

Izabella Goodair (12)
Lincoln Castle Academy, Lincoln

The Lights Dim Out

Dear Diary,

Today was average at minimum. Waking, I felt disrupted, livid and overall unsatisfied. Packing my things, I headed out to scavenge what was remaining of my working, thinking mind. As my eyes wandered, they fell down a luxurious mountain to see Odeon.

I strolled in, immediately hearing 'The Husher', a nicknamed killer who does what he wants. The screams of the characters echoed in my head thousands of times then snap. My eyes turned bright red like lava and he returned. The children behind me did not return that night. He struck in the open. Average day indeed.

Mason Lunn (13)

Lincoln Castle Academy, Lincoln

Guilty

"Guilty!" said the judge whilst slamming his hammer.
The devious robber turned white as snow.
"All that you have stolen shall go to those who you stole
from!" furiously said the judge.
The criminal broke down in tears as his knees collapsed.
"Please, please, please!" said the criminal while being
dragged out of the courtroom.
We all thought they had found the criminal after a month. I
wasn't completely sure they had found the criminal. He
seemed to be somewhere in his forties. He couldn't rob a full-
sized mansion by himself.

Zain Ahmed (12)
Lincoln Castle Academy, Lincoln

My Best Friend's Death

People think the dead can't talk but I think differently. My best friend died, and I was crying for hours. Three days passed, I was looking in the mirror and he appeared. I asked him, "Who killed you?" and he told me. I couldn't believe it. My dad walked into my room and cried, "Downstairs now." I looked at him in fear, turned to the mirror and my best friend was there, he looked at my dad in anger. I went to court and told them who killed my best friend. He said to me, "You will pay."

Alvin Nicholas-Iyoha (12)
Lincoln Castle Academy, Lincoln

The Unknown Murderer

"It just doesn't add up..." I said. "These clues make no sense." I smelt the rotten smell again. "What could it be?" I carried on walking and saw a bleeding head in the bin. "What happened?" I wondered. I went to look for clues but there was none. Usually, there would be some clues... wouldn't there? "This is all so confusing!" There it was again... A gunshot. My heart skipped a beat. "I should get out of here." I ran into an abandoned shed and leaned against the door. Banging over and over again... It stopped...

Ella Parkinson (12)
Lincoln Castle Academy, Lincoln

Kill The Founder

The sound of sobs travelled through the air as the moon illuminated the forest below. Dark red stained the blades of grass as warm hands held cold ones. Salty tears tumbled onto the mangled corpse sprawled across the floor. Cold air pierced his skin as he stared down at the motionless body - cradling it in his arms, almost like a mother would do to their child. Although, this wasn't the case. The thick, metallic stench was all he could smell - constantly reminding him. A piece of crumbled-up paper lay beside him, scribbled words being written down. 'Kill the founder'.

Alannah Maddock (12)
Lincoln Castle Academy, Lincoln

No Evidence

It didn't add up. Constantly closed, reopened, closed and reopened. I needed to get to the bottom of this. None of it made sense, hundreds of files with no definitive evidence. Knives with dried blood, no DNA retrieved from the attacker and no witnesses. Coincidence? I think not. As I looked further through the files I found that Lieutenant Weaver (a deserter from the army) deserted the day after the colonel was stabbed. What was going on? As I looked some more I found that Corporal Brandon, who was Weaver's best friend, was also killed. Some mysteries are never solved.

Matthew Kilby (11)
Lincoln Castle Academy, Lincoln

Don't Go Into The Woods

Walks in the woods. Relaxing, peaceful. Little did I know tonight wasn't. I was in the nearby forest in my neighbourhood, grass brushing against my ankles, backpack strapped to me. It wasn't until I came to an opening did things escalate. I caught something shiny in the grass, instinct telling me to investigate.

It was a knife, drawing in a sea of blood. Parting the leaves ahead, I walked straight into a murder scene. The culprit was gone. It was in the mud.

Sirens rang. Officers screamed. Seconds later, and I was in the back of a car in handcuffs...

Holly Breese (14)
Lincoln Castle Academy, Lincoln

Could It?

I woke up surrounded by tall trees overlooking me. It was a full moon, not a star in sight. In the distance, among a thick layer of fog was a tall, arched, stone gate. I could just make out what was engraved on it: 'Beware'.

Snap! I turned with caution. A stick must've been snapped. I wasn't alone... Who was there? What was there? Why? Was I trespassing? Why was this happening to me? *Snap!* Again but in a different direction? I turned quickly to see a faint outline of...

I woke up. A dream? No... It couldn't have been...

Amy Laughton (15)
Lincoln Castle Academy, Lincoln

I'm About To Blow

A man entered a bus. He entered with a vest. He said, "Nobody move or I'm going to blow this bus up."
People sat down and stayed quiet until someone asked what his name was.
"Buzz," he replied.
About three minutes later, the police arrived at the scene and were shocked by the scene that was happening on the bus. The officer called for backup. Once the terrorist saw this, he got the switch and shouted, "I'm about to blow!"
The vest failed and everyone cheered as the bus pulled over and let everyone out of it.

Filip Szmerdt (14)
Lincoln Castle Academy, Lincoln

Robbery Of Life And The Gift Of Death

Bang! The ear-shattering gunshot rang through the dark. The scream made my skin crawl.

The lights switched back on and he was lying there with the gun placed in his hand, dead. He was dead. Just as he was reading the will. But where was it gone? It had vanished. Everyone was standing in disbelief. How? Why? Who? People were in a state of frozen shock. Accusing eyes darted across the old room. John who stood to inherit looked in disbelief. "My money," he muttered. Aunty Mary looked at him in disgust. Then we noticed, where was Pete?

Archie Carter (15)
Lincoln Castle Academy, Lincoln

Innocent

Guilty! The gavel hit the podium. My heart sank. Found guilty of a crime I didn't commit, how?

My husband was murdered four years ago. The police were sure the case would go cold; it didn't.

I sat in my cell, staring at the wall wondering how this could happen when the buzzer sounded. The door swung open. Two men marched in and grabbed me, their grip deadly. They dragged me down the hall, shoved me into a dark room and left.

It was silent but then a light flickered on. A man appeared. "We know you're innocent," he grinned.

Darcie Chappell (14)
Lincoln Castle Academy, Lincoln

Death At Night

7:30pm. It's a dark and dreary night but something is different. A body, male. 5 foot 10 inches. Well, what the other officers suspect.

I look at the body and I examine the deadly injury. It was the neck, fresh blood still dripping and seeping through the cloth over him. I look at the weapon used to take this man's life. It's a kitchen knife. We examine it and it shows traces of other people's blood, some of whom are missing.

Then my radio comes to life. Four more dead bodies in Joe's Bar. The suspect killer - Dale Timer...

Theo Goodlass (15)
Lincoln Castle Academy, Lincoln

Vanishing Girls

It doesn't make any sense. All of these girls, disappearing without a trace. It started back in 2007, that was two years ago and the teenagers are still vanishing. Everything has gone cold, mainly the case. One by one, each month a fifteen-year-old perishes.

We only have one message from the kidnapper yet we still can't find the culprit. I have been trying but I still cannot find anything. It's like the girls were never in the records. I've asked a lot of people but I still have not got a proper lead. But little do they know...

Eli Cernoguzova (12)

Lincoln Castle Academy, Lincoln

The Suspect Was Gone

The suspect was gone! The room, a dark echo. A maze of screams and cries. Blood, limbs everywhere. It still haunts me, those poor souls. In the bathroom, a leg. In the kitchen, a hand. It was like a bear had entered the room. There was a bitter iron smell. The walls washed red. The white carpet stained. The ceiling cracked and caving in. Mould crawled around me, strangling me, suffocating me.

Suddenly, I fell to my knees. A random waft of emotion came over me. The orphanage, empty. The feeling of tight hugs surrounded me. The suspect was gone!

Nicole Burrows (13)
Lincoln Castle Academy, Lincoln

Breaking Point

I had an alibi, I promised the detective stood in my dorm surrounded by torn-apart corpses, even some pulled from under the sparkling floorboards. I was shocked. I don't understand what happened. It was really the worst day for this, I had to study for my biggest exam, yet they were saying I did it.

People walking past the door whispered about how they knew I would snap. I didn't do it! I explained everything to the detectives, maybe in a bit too much detail, to the point they didn't believe me.

This better be a dream... Ugh!

Alice Bingham (13)
Lincoln Castle Academy, Lincoln

Blue Lights

The rain angrily hit the floor. The blue lights flashed furiously. In this time of fear, the only thing saving my future was hiding. Jumping fences, jumping gates, I knew there was no hope in my mates.

The flashbacks of his body dropping down to the floor and the teardrops in his eyes. It scared me. It petrified me.

The only thing I could see was blue flashing lights. I just wanted money. Why did I get into this? *I'm not afraid to die*, rushed through my head. The blue lights flashed furiously. The rain angrily hit the floor.

Macy Loxley (15)
Lincoln Castle Academy, Lincoln

The Bang

As I walked around the park, *bang!* The massive statue in the centre of the park snapped in two. How? There was no one around. "How? What?" I spoke, questioning. What was going on? I was shocked. Was it on purpose? Did someone chop it or was it a ghost? I would never know.
Wait! What was there? I rushed to see... "Oh!" I gasped. I shook as I saw a person under it. Was I hallucinating?
She was still breathing, just hurt badly. She tried and tried but she just about told me her name. "Jenny," she said.

Krystal Gunner (12)
Lincoln Castle Academy, Lincoln

Dead Or Alive?

People think the dead can't talk. Is this a myth or not? On 23rd September 2004, I stood in a graveyard when the clock struck twelve. As I meandered through the intimidating, eerie graveyard, I heard a whisper linger throughout my ears. "Be careful," something mumbled. Again and again, it became louder. I tried to ignore it and kept on walking. But all I could think about was, could it be a spirit? My jaw dropped after seeing a gravestone saying 'Ellie Lewis died 31st October 2021'. What does this mean? Am I dead or alive?

Ellie Lewis (11)
Lincoln Castle Academy, Lincoln

Till This Day...

Rain punched my window. Lightning lit up the dark sky. I sat there at my desk, thinking back to an unsolved crime. I was so... angry with myself because I just couldn't figure it out. How did they do it? Why would they do it? I just didn't understand. I've been researching a lot about this crime. I still want to solve it but I just can't. I want to know what the killer's motive was.

I was looking through witness reports when I found this one. I couldn't remember reading it when the crime happened. Then it hit me...

Evie Richardson (13)

Lincoln Castle Academy, Lincoln

The Murder

People think the dead can't talk. We were walking through the graveyard and we saw a creepy abandoned house. My friend and I said, "Let's go." *Ding-dong.* We knocked on the door. It opened creakily by itself. It was dark. I saw a blood trail. I went in and the door slammed behind me and my friend. The door wouldn't open so I followed the blood trail. There were bodies everywhere. A man heard us and he started choking my friend. I called the police and hid. The police arrested the man. My friend died but I got out.

Chester Green (12)

Lincoln Castle Academy, Lincoln

The Final One

On a rainy day, me and my crew are ready. We jump out of the van, load the guns and run in.

"Everyone, get down!" I shout. Everyone drops. My buddy runs for the vault and places the explosives on it. *Boom!* We're in. We all run for the vault.

Someone presses the alarm. I turn and shoot him several times. He drops.

Ten minutes later, the SWAT team came busting in, taking down two of my buddies.

Me and my buddy run to the roof. We're trapped so I do the only possible thing. I shoot him and myself.

Cameron Wade (15)
Lincoln Castle Academy, Lincoln

Hello Mother

It just didn't add up, one minute my dearest daughter was lying in her bed, the next, gone! I was in utter shock. My heart dropped as tears welled up in my eyes. It all happened in a flash, the police, the sirens. Everything was a blur. The next day, Ella was all over the news, a search party was sent out in the town, but my poor baby girl was still missing. Then, a shadow at the door. Ella! Ella? She stood in the doorframe, tears rolling down her face, her clothes dripping in scarlet-red blood. "Hello, Mother..."

Lily Esberger (11)
Lincoln Castle Academy, Lincoln

Revealed

Bang! The gunshots sounded. The police were called to screaming and crying in the tallest building in Europe but there was no man in sight, just a stream of blood flowing out of the locked room. The only known person to have access to the key was known to be aggressive and not let anyone near that key.

The police got back-up to knock the door down. They arrived and were ready to find out this mystery.

After a long thirty minutes, they found out who it was.

Bang! The gavel in the courtroom echoed.

Oliver Lacey (13)

Lincoln Castle Academy, Lincoln

Unexpected Visitor

"Guilty!" I had been convicted for a crime I didn't do. "I sentence you to death by lethal injection!"
Every bit of hope I had of being found innocent was lost, gone, never to come back until... now. I have two weeks until I'm dead. I stood and started to pace around my cell, waiting for my inevitable death. The cell opened and I was taken to the visitation room. I saw a man in a hoodie covering his face. He sat down. He looked up, I was shocked! It was the man I supposedly killed. He set me up!

Mason Cordell (12)
Lincoln Castle Academy, Lincoln

He's Watching You

He's always watching, lurking in the shadows, tapping on your window. His smirk is cold and deep, leaving chills shivering through your body. Do not look at him. His looks even kill. His watch ticks slowly and rehearsed. His victim's scream is muffled by fabric. A painful torture, finishing by burning them. No one's able to find him. Not a single trace. He runs and disappears. Don't follow his trail. He's always watching. He's never been caught. Don't look out your window, he's watching you...

Grace Clipsham (14)
Lincoln Castle Academy, Lincoln

Death Is Sour

People think the dead can't talk but I will in the afterlife. I was strapped into the electric chair, the embodiment of the Grim Reaper standing next to the button to kill me. A glass panel ten metres in length stops me from being with my family. I could see my family crying, my grandmother ran out of the room in mourning. I could see my friends sitting around in their best clothes and I could see my twin brother... smirking. He set me up. He faked his own death. He ruined my life. I'm going to kill that monster!

Josh Myhill (13)
Lincoln Castle Academy, Lincoln

The Exorcism

The exorcism was about to begin. However, it wasn't the usual priest performing the exorcism. It was a ghost hunter. And so it began. The girl in question was tied down with thick chains. The ghost hunter drew a ring around her with gold ink as I watched on. Suddenly, she broke free of her bonds and flew savagely at the man. She slammed into him and started nailing long, rusted spikes through his hands, shins and collarbones. The exorcism failed. I ran. No looking back. I never thought my sister would try to kill me.

Abigail Clarke (13)
Lincoln Castle Academy, Lincoln

The Shadow

Feeling a shiver down my spine, fear tingled through my body. I took a step closer, placing the flowers down. I then heard a voice and felt myself drop to the floor. 3am. I looked around and saw I wasn't at a graveyard. I was in a building that looked like a haunted, abandoned, dirty house. There was a single door in front of me and a shadow beside it. It came closer and whispered something in my ear. I couldn't work out what it was saying. The shadow placed its hands on my shoulders and started to clench them.

Shyla Stewart (12)

Lincoln Castle Academy, Lincoln

The Startling Stroll

The rain was falling and the lightning struck. The streets of Manchester were dull and the street lights were flickering. Me and my mum went for a walk down the river at 6pm. My mum said she was going to get some wood for the fire and told me to keep walking.

Time flew by and it ended up to be 7pm. I started to call my mum's name but she wouldn't answer. The horror sent shivers down my spine and sweat dripped down my face. *Bang!* I heard a gunshot. My mum! Was she still breathing? Or not...

Lucy Matchett (13)

Lincoln Castle Academy, Lincoln

The Wrong Decision

A shadow at the door was the last thing I saw before disaster struck. It started when my daughter, Sarah, was begging me to play with her, but it was almost impossible when she made a blood-curdling scream. I shouted to her to play with someone else which would be the worst decision I've ever made. Shortly after, I noticed a shadow much bigger than my daughter on the outside of my front door. I rushed after whatever that was, but when I opened the front door, my daughter and whatever that was, was already gone.

Mohamed Bridan (12)
Lincoln Castle Academy, Lincoln

Unsolved

"Guilty!" Let's go back a bit. The murder happened on Grayhamn Street of Amanda Clograine, but her body was missing. There were three suspects and they thought it was me since I 'escaped prison'. The lie detector results were back... disastrous! I was being framed! I was 'lying' about liking tuna, that wasn't a question. They thought it was me because I'm a 'serial killer'. I just hope that they don't find the actual serial killer's body that I actually killed.

Willow Reid (12)
Lincoln Castle Academy, Lincoln

Sleepover

Gloomy, dark sky. Light coming from the TV. Reaching my hand into my bag, pulling out my sharp, shiny knife. Seeing myself in the reflection of the knife. Piercing the knife into the three girls' chests. Two down... One down... Dark red blood splatters onto the white walls. The smell of fresh blood fills my nose.

As I stand up fixing my hair, in the corner of my eye I see a red flash behind the curtains. I slowly walk over and grab it. I turn it over to find out it has been recording me the whole time...

Viktoria Jakovleva (15)
Lincoln Castle Academy, Lincoln

Alibi

I had an alibi. I had told the judge my alibi but they lied. He said he was with another friend of his and they agreed. "Guilty!" shouted the judge. Then my 'alibi' laughed along with his friend as I was taken away. When I was thrown into my cell I realised it was all a trick. He was distracting me to let his friend get away with murder. Their laughter echoed in my ears as I sat there in my cell for a murder I didn't do, trapped in an old uncomfortable cell... I will get my revenge... soon.

Chelsey Newton (12)

Lincoln Castle Academy, Lincoln

The Missing

On this day one year ago a twelve-year-old girl was kidnapped. She still hasn't been found. Now my job is to find her. I won't let this case go cold. This girl needs to be home with her family. This case isn't like any others. We have no clues.

That was until an anonymous message was sent. It is coordinates, not too far from where the girl was last seen. It could just be a fake message to throw us off, but we're not taking any chances. Although this can put myself in danger, she is in more.

Summer Lloyd (14)
Lincoln Castle Academy, Lincoln

An Army Pilot's Disaster

I set off on my third and final mission, soaring through the air faster than the speed of sound, flying over Europe. I was enjoying my last flight as I'd be retiring this year.

As I was flying over the beautiful mountain range of Italy, I noticed something. My jet was plummeting to the ground! I slowed the jet down as much as I could until I was so close to the ground. I leapt out of my jet mid-air... Luckily, I had a parachute, however, someone had switched it with a backpack. I was most likely dead.

Jack Johnson (12)
Lincoln Castle Academy, Lincoln

The Heist

It is time, time for the heist. I gathered everyone up. I uncovered the tunnel to London and hundreds of armed men marched through to England's money factory where it all began. Good luck. Once we arrived, we opened fire! *Bang! Bang!* Most of the factory workers were dead but the police were on their way, so we quickly gathered the money and got out of there. The police beat us to it and most of us were arrested or killed. I slipped away with £37,000,000. I had succeeded but at what cost?

Adam Blaszkiewicz (12)
Lincoln Castle Academy, Lincoln

Dead

It was 8:30 hours and I was making breakfast for my cousins. When I called out to them, all I heard was absolute silence which got me instantly worried. Without hesitation, I made my way to their bedroom and what I saw sent a wave of fear through my veins. There was blood everywhere. No sign of weapons anywhere. Just my two cousins lying on the bed: dead. I could hardly move. I knew I had to do something but my brain kept screaming at me, "They're dead, they're dead, they're dead..."

Jesse Osaje (12)
Lincoln Castle Academy, Lincoln

Nefarious

I was in Zemblanity when I discovered she was killed, but I felt almost relieved to be exonerated of the wrongdoings I had to withstand. She then destroyed everything when she decided to escape and now I was getting framed for murdering my mother. Now I was a 'nefarious girl', a gratuitous murderer. I began to tear as I realised what the judge had said. Guilty. I felt myself being pulled away from where I stood. Looking up, I saw my mother with a charmolypi look as she quickly fled apathetically.

Erin Mallard (12)
Lincoln Castle Academy, Lincoln

Guilty!

Guilty! It was confirmed. He did it or did he? CCTV says he was there but half the workers said he wasn't there. Was he at the restaurant or did he rob the bank? The lie detector said he was telling the truth, he wasn't there but how did CCTV and some workers see him at the restaurant? They tried to find him on the system but he wasn't on it. The workers didn't know who he was and the CCTV didn't show him there anymore, only the police remembered him. It was like he didn't exist.

Riley Langridge (13)
Lincoln Castle Academy, Lincoln

Injustice

I stand trial in front of a court for murder. The judge and jury all made their decision. Without saying anything, I can see it in their faces. It's obvious. I didn't murder anybody but I still face trial.

It all happened at night two days ago. When I got back from my job I was tired and ready to go to sleep and then I heard my stairs creak. I didn't think anything of it until I heard breathing. I turned around and nothing was there. I turned back and it was standing in front of me...

Ashton Gillyett (15)

Lincoln Castle Academy, Lincoln

A Shadow At The Door

A shadow at the door. "Hello," I said. The shadow got smaller. It went up the hallway and back out the door. I ran after it. Blinding green light lit up my front garden. Many small green men ran at my ankles until there was enough of them to drag my ankles and my body into the light. Was I dying? I passed out and ended up in a room in a cold, dark, empty room. Once again, there was a shadow in the door. It came into the light and it was like looking in a mirror. "That's crazy!"

Ruari Sheeran (13)
Lincoln Castle Academy, Lincoln

The Crazy House

There was a new mission to start. The murder of a mother who worked at home with a loving family. But this didn't add up. At 11:55am the family was outside but then we got told by the father and plumber that they thought the crime happened at about 12pm. We got there at 12:30pm and the blood looked about twenty minutes old. The father said he heard a loud scream, but the only person outside was the child. He was asked questions but didn't answer any. This was my hardest mission yet...

Emily Cierpka (12)
Lincoln Castle Academy, Lincoln

I Got Scratched By A Ghost

I am a detective. My name is Kacie and I had been set on a mission to search a house for clues of a murderer.
As I stepped into the house I heard a noise, a noise that I thought was the trees but later on found out it was something else. Leaving the door open was a bad idea. Walking into the dining room, the front door slammed. Panic hit.
Checking if the door had locked, I felt a shiver down my spine and heard an unusual sound. Unlocking the door, I saw a long scratch down my back.

Kacie Clarke (12)
Lincoln Castle Academy, Lincoln

The Clue

I found a clue that is leading to my final answer which I have been looking for. Now I just need the camera's password to find the killer of my friend. Aha, the password's 2829. Wait, this all doesn't add up. At the time my friend was killed the killer was nowhere to be seen. What do I do? My brain is in pieces like a puzzle where you don't know what to do. Aha, now I know what to do. I can do a DNA test on the weapon they were killed with. Now it's all coming together...

Kian Robinson (12)

Lincoln Castle Academy, Lincoln

The Poisoned Coma

My dad fell into a coma with no evidence of why. As I was visiting him in the hospital, my dad started clicking his fingers but I thought it was muscle memory. But no. It kept happening over and over with stops in between and the same pattern.

One day, I decided to see if it was Morse Code to see if it spelt out anything. What it spelt out shocked me to the core... It said, 'I was poisoned in my food by...' *By who?* I thought. Who had done this? I had to find out...

Isabelle Keating (12)
Lincoln Castle Academy, Lincoln

The Chase

Hi, I'm Jake. I'm an FBI agent and I'm on a mission to find a lost criminal. He has stolen all the diamonds in London and hidden them. I have to find them.

I find three in a building, three in a tree and finally three at the start of a wood. I'm going to go in! The criminal must have gone this way but dropped the diamonds.

As I walk through the woods I see the guy behind this crime but he sees me too. He runs as fast as he can so he gets away. Maybe next time.

Alfie Middlebrook (12)

Lincoln Castle Academy, Lincoln

The Missing Boys

It just didn't add up, why did their parents let them go to the lake? Why were their clothes there and why was their blood on the tree? Where did they go? Did they drown or did they get kidnapped? I guess we'll never know... I've found a clue! I did it, I know where they've gone. It all makes sense, the blood on the tree, the clothes and why they were unsupervised. After the home inspection, it was clear they were being neglected. They must have escaped or have they...?

Chloe Delaney (11)
Lincoln Castle Academy, Lincoln

The Suspect

"The suspect is gone!" exclaimed the chief of operations.
"What?"
"A vicious criminal, a serial killer broke out of solitary confinement yesterday at 12am. We must find him immediately!" screamed the warden in a shrill voice.
"Yes Sir," he said.
Two days later, a dead body was brought to the attention of the police. The body had a knife with the words, 'I told you I would be back'. The figure was emblazoned onto it...

Callum Purkis (12)
Lincoln Castle Academy, Lincoln

The House Past The Hill

One night I stayed at my grandad's house and he told a story about the house past the hill. Harry and Bill lived near a hill but were forbidden from going past. They never knew why and they joked they would die. One day, their parents were out and they decided to go over the hill. Harry and Bill were never seen again.

The next day my brother Jack and I decided to visit the well on the hill. Jack went first while I got some drinks. I came outside to see he was gone. I woke up.

Leo Sawyer (12)
Lincoln Castle Academy, Lincoln

The Closed Case

All the evidence pointed to suicide but something didn't add up. The body was discovered at the base of a skyscraper. The day of the death the camera at the top of the skyscraper broke. They had no suspects. They had no concrete evidence. If they had nothing by the end of the day it would be declared a suicide and the case would be closed. The clock tower chimed. It was now midnight. Time was up. They declared the case closed. The lead detective left grinning. He had got away...

Ollie Smith (12)
Lincoln Castle Academy, Lincoln

Date With Destiny

It was my first day as the lead detective and my first case was a cold case - a missing person! A girl who had been on a date with an ex-criminal was now missing. The only evidence was CCTV footage of them having a good time and the dress she was wearing.

Back to now. I am on a date (undercover) with the suspect but I have backup. One hour later, we arrive at his apartment and I am hit with perfume. He says, "I have a surprise." I see all of the missing girls ever.

Bethany Hewson (14)
Lincoln Castle Academy, Lincoln

Missing Person

It just didn't add up. He was sitting in the restaurant and all of a sudden he was gone. All his food was still on the table. I was perplexed. He wasn't in the toilet. He wasn't in the car park. He was just gone. All we could find was footsteps of blood leading to the door. The flashing lights of the police car told everyone to get on the floor. As I lay on the floor I looked to my right and saw the remains of the missing person under the table. I was in shock.

Lily-Mae Fearon (12)
Lincoln Castle Academy, Lincoln

People Think The Dead Can't Talk

People think the dead can't talk, but I do. One morning, I awoke slowly, to smell a rotten corpse. I was asleep for two days, as I was ill. I slowly got up to see my sister's dead body covered in stab wounds and blood. My mouth dropped and my heart stopped. I tried to talk, but I was in shock. That was seven years ago, but I still wonder who did this to her or should I say me? I was the sister who was stabbed and cut. All that I had said came from my living sister.

Lani Johnson (11)
Lincoln Castle Academy, Lincoln

The Hotel Massacre

I see her. She walks up the stairs to the second floor of the hotel. I follow. I am a few metres behind. She gets her room key out. I can't help but follow her in. I run and cover her mouth. She screams and tries to bite my hand. She passes out. I walk over to the door and close it. I remember I have a knife in the pocket of my ragged jeans. I get it out. I click the button to open it. I can't help myself. I run the blade along her stomach. Red blood pours.

Penny Hatton (12)

Lincoln Castle Academy, Lincoln

Finally Guilty

In the courtroom the room was silent. I was in tears of joy! I had solved the mystery and he was guilty! It had been five whole years without justice but then I looked up and saw a familiar face. It was him! He was still on the loose and I wasn't going to let this slide so I dashed out of the door and the chase was on. I wouldn't let him get away with the mass murder he had committed. After a long period of fatigued running a confused face was on the floor.

Jack Cartwright (12)
Lincoln Castle Academy, Lincoln

The Figure

It was 2am. A knock came on my front door. I went downstairs to check it out, I was shaking... A weird shadow stood at my front door holding what seemed to be a weapon of some sort. I opened the door, nothing was there except a note which read 'Turn around'. When I saw this figure my soul left my body and I froze into place. This was no monster. It was a big hairy beast. I ran outside as fast as I could but the more I ran the closer he got so I hid...

Cody Durrance (12)
Lincoln Castle Academy, Lincoln

The Lies

I sat there pleading to the court that I hadn't killed my only friend in this world, but I knew who did. Her mischievous smirk made my blood boil; the fake tears running down her face were annoyingly believable. I knew the truth and I needed to get justice for my friend. The judge said, "The jury is ready to deliberate." Suddenly, there was a verdict; the court rose but I couldn't. My body froze, with sweat dripping down my face anxiously...

Kyla Cassell (13)
Lincoln Castle Academy, Lincoln

The Lie Detector Test

Five weeks ago my uncle died but I'm going to get my revenge... I have got three suspects and the lie detector results are back. Turns out they all didn't do it but someone knows who did. As I retested them all I was right, it was not any of them. All along they have been innocent. Who killed him wasn't even a surprise. The lie detector was rigged. It was the lie detector guy but he luckily escaped. He won't be this lucky for long though.

Matas Ulkstinas (13)

Lincoln Castle Academy, Lincoln

Guilty!

Guilty! Or is he? Only he and his lawyer knew if he was guilty or not. If he admitted to killing two people he would only get three years but if he lied he would get six years. No one had found the bodies so the guard took him back to his cell but as he was walking back two girls lowered their sunglasses a little bit. "I knew it, they set me up. I'm going to kill them," he said as the guard took him back to his cell.

Brody Ballard (12)
Lincoln Castle Academy, Lincoln

The Hotel Room

It was a Saturday night, I got called to clean room 66. As I made my way over to the room, a creepy man walked behind me. I got my room key and opened the door. I screamed. The man covered my mouth and I passed out. A policeman barged through the door and tasered the man, cuffing him. The man pulled something from his pocket and sprayed it in the officer's face. The man then made his escape through the window.

Abigail Parks (12)

Lincoln Castle Academy, Lincoln

The Mystery

It just doesn't make sense. We chased him. We followed him from the house he stole from yet ten minutes later we found him in a car. The confusing part is he was there for twenty minutes. We know this because of his camera. We took him to the station but his alibi was too good. After that, we could only question him and let him go which we did. He left laughing as his brother got away because of him.

Oliver Key (12)
Lincoln Castle Academy, Lincoln

Run!

I ran. I ran as fast as I could. I felt like I was flying. I was running so fast it felt like my face was melting. I hid behind a tall, gloomy, oddly shaped bush. "Becca!" I heard them shout, but I stayed quiet. I can't believe I shot him. I shot him, finally after all the trauma he's caused me... I'm free. I can't believe I can say that. I'm free!

Bianca Preda (14)
Lincoln Castle Academy, Lincoln

The Man Who Loves To Kill

1998, I came home to policemen, caution tape and a crime scene. Blood on the wall, blood on the floor, blood on the roof and blood on the door. Five bloody potato sacks containing five bloody bodies. I look outside the window with blood dripping from the window frame, Kye the Ripper is covered in blood and holding a bloody knife and smiling like pain brings him joy!

Matthew Achanso Tamanji (12)

Lincoln Castle Academy, Lincoln

The Delivery Man

The day was dark and gloomy. The delivery man walked up to the old, mysterious door. He opened the door; it creaked. The man heard a giggle coming from upstairs and the door locked shut. The lights started to flicker. They suddenly went out. He saw a smile coming from the stairs and the pointy tip of the blade. It was over.

Jayden Wilmer (14)
Lincoln Castle Academy, Lincoln

The Unsolved Mystery

In the moonlit grove, a clandestine gathering commenced. Whispers, thick with trepidation, permeated the air, as each attendee cast wary glances at the others. The conductor of this enigmatic symphony, a figure shrouded in darkness, held aloft a jewel-encrusted chalice.

"The elixir," they murmured, "unveils the forbidden path." With trembling hands, the chalice was raised to quivering lips and the nectar consumed. Transfixed, the guests awaited enlightenment, but chaos erupted instead. Silent screams echoed through the grove as one by one, they vanished into thin air, leaving behind only the chilling enigma of their inexplicable disappearance.

The mystery remains unsolved.

Aayan Malik (15)
Littleover Community School, Littleover

Crime After Crime

Some people have secrets and there are those who have deadly secrets.

The screaming silence filled my ears, raucous rain thundered. I knew what she'd done. I knew what had to be done. I screamed...

"How... Why?

"Laura, I can explain..."

"Explain what? Your lies, secrets? I'm done and ending this tonig-..."

"No!" she bellowed, grasping me tightly...

I screamed, ripping her claws off me, throwing her down, her head hitting the jagged rocks as she fell....

Some people have secrets and there are those who have deadly secrets. I just didn't know one of those people would be me...

Vanessa Lezama (12)
Littleover Community School, Littleover

Unstoppable

She is unknown. Looks ordinary; she is not. Eyes as green as emeralds and hair as orange as fire. She is not what she portrays. Only her victims know she is a heartless witch, devouring children day and night while enjoying each petite piece. Child after child disappears; innocent parents not knowing and blaming themselves.

Unfortunately, there is nothing anyone can do to stop this savage woman. Her real form is purely evil, however, only I knew.

I was almost devoured, but I escaped luckily and my mobile device saved me.

Beware! She is scarily unstoppable. Dangerously unstoppable. Unstoppable...

Shereen Aslam (15)
Littleover Community School, Littleover

The Bloody Corpse

Detective Maryam sighed as she walked along the dull, narrow alleyway. Her job had finished and she was now redundant. What would she do? There was nothing left for her in this lonely city.

She continued walking and decided to take a different route back to her house today. Suddenly, she almost tripped over something... a knife! With blood dripping from it! She slowly looked to her left, a body lying on the floor.... motionless.

She instantly recognised the face of the corpse, Miss Smith, the deputy headmistress of her old school! She observed the corpse cautiously for any evidence...

Haniyah Shakeb (12)

Littleover Community School, Littleover

The Bank Robbery

Detective Mason entered the bank, his keen eyes scanning the scene. Gunmen, hidden behind masks, held terrified hostages at gunpoint. Instinct took over as he swiftly disarmed the first gunman, firing a precise shot. Chaos erupted as the sound of gunfire echoed through the bank. Detective Mason, now a hero, had neutralised any threats and carried hostages to safety. It was in the moments later however as police entered that another crime was committed. Vaults had been broken into, though no gunmen left with the money. 50 million dollars had vanished, and at the same time, so had the detective.

Abdur-Rahman Imran
Littleover Community School, Littleover

Innocent

I waited, restless, in my restraining cell. I shouldn't be in this prison block! I hadn't done anything wrong... I was being convicted for a crime that I did not commit. My conscience was clean and my hands had no staining.

It felt like I was being tormented: I had nothing to do but soliloquise on my undeniable innocence.

Finally, the forensic scientist was back with his chromatography paper, to prove that that ink sample was not mine.

He approached. He leant forward. He grabbed my collar. My neck was injected and I fell face flat.

Joseph Law (13)
Littleover Community School, Littleover

My Best Friend

Dead. Killed. Who could it be? I look around the room for any evidence. The only thing I find is blood. Everywhere. I need to tell someone. But at the same time, I need to know who killed my best friend. But she wasn't my 'best' friend. She was controlling. She used me. She lied to me. But she still said she loved me. Who could have done this? This sinful act.

I need to find out who it was and get vengeance. There wasn't enough time for us. We weren't meant to be. Turns out I killed her.

Alishah Raja (14)

Littleover Community School, Littleover

My Dead Friend

They say the dead are supposed to stay dead. I thought that too at first but I guess I was wrong... very wrong. She died in my arms. So, tell me, how is she walking in through the front door - alive? No words escaped her mouth, she walked right past me. I cried out to her but still no response.

I screamed her name at the top of my lungs and then she disappeared as if she was never there. The door opened once more, she was back again.

The same thing kept repeating over and over again like clockwork.

Holly Gibbon (14)
Littleover Community School, Littleover

Once A Thief

"There it is," says Sam.

"Yeah, the Rossi estate," says Nate.

"Let's run through the plan. We climb in and cut the electric and Sully steals the Golden Cross of Dismas."

As the brothers Sam and Nate climb through the window for the electric room, they encounter a problem. It's locked. Luckily, they pick the lock and get in. Once they cut the lights, Sully runs, takes the cross and makes his escape. Nate and Sam climb over the roof and jump down to the road where the car awaits. They drive to the distance with glee.

Archie Davidson (13)
Pentrehafod School, Hafod

Meal Deal Swapped

It just didn't add up. Who'd do such a thing? Who would swap my cheese meal deal for a ham meal deal? I reckon it was George Whale, he's known for it!

I reported it to the police. They said, "Sorry, ma'am, it wasn't George Whale." They didn't find him. So who is my suspect? OMG, the police just told me that they found my meal deal! They told me that they would do fingerprints so they could find the criminal.

It is now a month later and still no news. I talked to the police but there's no use!

Eva Young (11)
Pentrehafod School, Hafod

Hard Evidence

People think the dead can't talk but they can. Evidence speaks for the deceased. I'd found a knife within the body. The knife had fingerprints on it and I knew who had murdered him.

I carefully handed the evidence to the lead officer and told him, "Connor Richards did it."

I was the reason that Connor Richards was arrested and sentenced to death. I was the reason that Connor Richards is dead. All because of me. It was because of me that a man had died. Even if guilty, I felt remorse that I was the reason he was dead.

Owain Phillips (12)
Pentrehafod School, Hafod

No Name

People think the dead can't talk... The lead suspect, Alistair Morgan. The victim, a little girl, 'no name'. I'm the detective. I've just started this case. The girl was eight years old, killed in an old playground.

But only I know this little girl left a trail like she knew she was gonna die. Two nights after this, the girl spoke to me. I realised something, my competition, Grayle... It was all too good to be true. I knew he had something to do with this. I know he did it... I just have to prove it...

Isabelle Whitefoot (13)

Pentrehafod School, Hafod

That One Sound

Guilty, I thought as the suspect started running. Alberto Chairingson, the man who did it all. I began chasing him but then he turned and got hit by a car. That's how Alberto Chairingson died to Leo Noodlebin.

A week later, while I was finishing my shift, I heard a sound in the staffroom. I went to investigate but the moment I got to the door it stopped... I walked away but I heard it again. So I grabbed my bat and ran to the staffroom and there he was, Alberto Chairingson, charging at me...

Jacob T Lewis (12)
Pentrehafod School, Hafod

Shadow Figure

I found myself in a familiar yet different place.
The only thing I possess is a memory. A memory of a
shadow figure marching slowly towards me. Then suddenly
everything went dark.
When I woke up I was lying in a room. It seemed familiar. I
don't know what it was, it just... was. Once I got a hold of
myself I rose from the bed and headed over to the vanity
mirror and what I saw was horrifying! I leapt back in horror
and ran as what I saw was a terrifying, disgusting human!

Charnia Wilshese-Butler (12)
Pentrehafod School, Hafod

120

The Crimson Print

A deafening scream came from the sinister room. Nobody dared to step in! The only thing left was an unsettling crimson print. Everyone started to suspect everyone like a crowd torturing someone. They all pointed at me... It felt like a group ridiculing me. The stunned detective locked in a mysterious investigation. The towering silhouettes around me had an alibi, all but one. The sight of fear made them smirk like they'd committed a crime. As the alleged murderer was caught and everyone left I let out a cunning and psychotic laugh knowing I was a free man without charges.

Alexander Wood (14)
Pyrland School, Taunton

Not-So-Great Escape

Bank robbery... Two people and a teller pleading for help.
Sometime later, *bang, bang.* Police rushed in and found a
robber in the vault. Minutes later, the police came out with
the suspect, pleading for his life. He said, "Please, I'm
innocent. I was in a pub. Check the CCTV. I was walking
around."
"He is correct."
When they weren't looking he made a run for it, hopping in
a car and driving away at high speed. He swung in and out
of cars cutting them up, finally crashing into a lamppost and
getting arrested after all.

Keiran Prince (13)
Pyrland School, Taunton

A Poisoning

A shadow at the door... I thought it was just me at home, but I guess not! I could hear footsteps and it felt like I was being watched. I took a sip of my drink. It was fine. I turned away for a second and took another sip of my drink. It tasted odd. I ended up falling to the ground in agony. The footsteps got a bit closer and closer... A faint whisper in my ear. I tried to call someone for help but a hand pulled my phone away. Unfortunately, I didn't stay alive, I died.

Ella Duheaume (13)

Pyrland School, Taunton

A Guilty Waltz

No one has noticed the two figures dancing through a putrid mound of corpses. The rancid scent of rotting flesh does not seem to bother either of the pair as they go spinning over the bloodstained cobbles, in fact, they enjoy the bittersweet taste of chaos on their tongues. Their peculiar sway continues, stepping past stray bodies. Who are they? Messengers of death? Or perhaps callous murderers? Hysterical grins have been carved into their sickly faces, concealed by a strange hollow darkness. Off they wander, although they both know this place well, night-time dancers among the stench of death itself.

Florence Haines (12)
St Gregory's Catholic College, Odd Down

Eight To One Big Issues

Eight teenagers from different family backgrounds went to a camp where they learnt how to live without money. One of them was a killer and was very manipulative. He killed six people out of the eight that went to the camp. In the end, the murderer was among the last two people (Derek and Daviun). Daviun was caught as he was chasing Derek out of the camp. Derek was fast enough to call the police and the police discovered that it was Daviun's parents who introduced him to exploiting rich people, killing their children and selling their belongings online.

Veritas Okokhere (13)

St Gregory's Catholic College, Odd Down

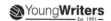
What Did I See?

Crash! My cloak hit the floor. My hands were shaking, it had been three hours and fifty-one minutes since the death of Kim Clarke. I had watched the entire scene and I knew what I saw. It was seven this morning when Kim got into her car, in a rush, and was about to start it, when a pick-up truck came speeding down the road. It reversed directly into Kim's car and crushed her to death. I had watched the murderer speed off into the distance and when their eyes met mine, I knew, I wouldn't sleep again...

Ayla Rowland (12)

St Gregory's Catholic College, Odd Down

Below The Night Sky

The lights of the city shone all around as the car drove down 5th. The night sky above, dark as ink, seemed so far above the illuminated skyscrapers. The car slowed. A woman got out, her black hair flowing down her back and a gun poised at her side. As the doors swung open, Daniel looked up. His eyes widened in utter terror as a gunshot broke the silence of the night. All he saw was a woman, with hair as black as death, running away down the steps of the hotel and the body of his father, lying there.

Tilly While (13)
St Gregory's Catholic College, Odd Down

What Happened In The Forest?

It just didn't make sense. No noise made. Attack from behind. No evidence left behind. The crime, a fatal stabbing. By now, I'd played it out hundreds of times in my head and still... no idea. How was all our evidence a sound recording from over twenty metres away? How did the attacker stay silent walking on the crackling branches and rustly leaves? What was the motive?

A distant voice called out to me. As usual, I'd fallen asleep on my desk. "Mr Tom Leverage, we believe we've found a key suspect. Age, 21. Name, William Leverage."

That's my brother...

Michal Chodurski (13)
St John Fisher Catholic Voluntary Academy, Dewsbury

Family Reunion Mystery

It wasn't adding up. The murder happened upstairs. All suspects were downstairs except us siblings. As the detective of the family, it was my job to investigate Dad's murder.

Most suspects had valid alibis except Deacon (my brother) and Darcy (my sister). They were both upstairs at the time of the murder, however, I had a hunch that Deacon was the main suspect. The more evidence I found the more I realised I knew nothing about my brother.

Our family reunion turned deadly when the body was discovered with a knife through its heart. From then on, everyone was suspect.

Safa Hussain (13)

St John Fisher Catholic Voluntary Academy, Dewsbury

I Didn't Expect It From You

Slowly, I glanced over at the bloodied knife on the kitchen counter. I took a deep breath. This was the fourth murder in a month and the killer was still out there.

I knew that the key to solving the case was in the victim's phone, but it was still locked. I called in the tech team and waited anxiously for them to crack the code.

Finally, after hours of work, they found a video that showed them the killer's face. I recognised the man immediately. It was my own partner. I had been working with the murderer all along.

Annie Dean (13)
St John Fisher Catholic Voluntary Academy, Dewsbury

Murder By The Pool

It just didn't add up. Every suspect had a watertight alibi. The more we searched the less evidence we could get. The street was blocked off so nothing could get moved or tampered with. Until we got to the end house, no rock was unturned and every letter they had was read.

Then a witness came forward but it was hard to understand. It was too hard to report. This rocked my world to the core. It was like a storm was cast over my head. The more I saw them, the more I was uneasy. It was my partner.

Caylass Toohey (13)
St John Fisher Catholic Voluntary Academy, Dewsbury

Bloody Melody

Shots and screams emerged from the dim audience, a jarring juxtaposition against the elegant melody playing. The stage light flickered. A couple of sparks flew from the darkness, rapidly igniting into a crackling flame that danced among the bleeding bodies. The theatre glowed; reds, oranges, yellows - all mixed in a bloody flurry of colours. People clambered against the crumbling furniture like zombies, hoping to escape the blazing inferno, despite already bearing wounds. 3am. Bursts of red bloomed from the tutus as blood seeped through. One by one the dancers all dropped to the floor, the fire licking against their skin.

Sophia Hermoso (13)
St Paul's Catholic College, Burgess Hill

My Family

Cowering under the blanket, shaking with tears, waiting for the screams to subside. Dad's home from the pub. He stepped through the door, Mum hurried me upstairs. She could tell by the weight of his footsteps and the furrow in his brow whether she should expect another black eye or not. The thudding and screaming became deafening, then silence. I crawled out of my faded Mickey Mouse covers and apprehensively crept down the stairs. Lying in a pool of blood, Mother's body draped across the bottom steps. I uncurled her fist to find a pocket knife. She wanted him dead.

Aleena Joseph (13)
St Paul's Catholic College, Burgess Hill

I Didn't Do It, It Wasn't Me

What is real? What is fake? There's a knife clenched in my shivering hand. My brother crawled up against the wall. Our eyes locked - tears pooling up. "Do it, kill him." The voice ran faster through my confused mind. I drew closer, my body trembling with every movement. My arm raised, his fear melted into cries. Still. Quiet. I ripped out the knife that was once clean, now covered in the life of my brother. What have I done? Why? I will never get him back. The blood fails to wash off. I didn't do this, it wasn't me. No.

Shreya Paul (13)
St Paul's Catholic College, Burgess Hill

Help

'Five years ago, twelve people disappeared in Sao Luis, Brazil. And I know w- end of transmission'.

Two years ago, today marks the anniversary of the independence of Guyana, and, of course, my birthday!

"That's what they always say. Never even a mention of the twelve. It's like the government pays them or something," said Vondila.

"That's a bit far-fetched, don't you think?" said Perdita.

"Hey, Perdita, I just looked up what our names mean and they are types of well, Perdita."

"What, Vondila? Vondila?" Where was he? "Vondila!" Then she saw. The laptop was smashed with one word. 'Help'.

Dylan Johnson-Middlehurst (12)
Ysgol John Bright, Llandudno

I Saw It!

Alone in the dark, I search the eerie school corridors, moving quickly through the darkness. I pray it doesn't find me.
The footsteps grow louder behind me until I feel its icy breath on my skin. I turn around slowly to face the thing and it says, "You forgot your homework."
"Argh! Wh-who are you?"
"I am the homework monster and I will eat your homework so you get negatives."
"No!"
"Yes!" *Omnomnom.*
I run as fast as I can along the corridor so it doesn't eat the rest of my homework. I turn left and then I see it...

Alana Owen (12)
Ysgol John Bright, Llandudno

Always Watching!

It was a regular day throughout town. The sun was gleaming down upon smiling faces, except for one. Joe just came back from a nightshift, with no one to come home to. Sighing, she opened up her phone, to a message saying, 'I'm always watching!' She screamed in horror, ran to her front door and slammed it shut. Locking it instantly.

Later that day, another message appeared on her phone. This time, she couldn't find the courage to open it. As she quivered another message popped up. She knew someone was watching her. *Knock!* Someone was at the door...

Holly Pitts (12)

Ysgol John Bright, Llandudno

Vault Robberies

Carl knew he'd done it. At 22:14hrs on the 7th of July, he'd broken into the bank and stolen £450,000 from Vault 2. He had a close call with a security guard outside Vault 1 but it was otherwise fine.

John knew he'd done it. At 22:13hrs on the 7th of July, he'd broken into the bank and stolen £450,000 from Vault 1. He had a close call with a security guard outside Vault 2 but it was otherwise fine.

"Interrogation concerning the robbery of Vaults 1 and 2 of Johnson's Bank on July 7th!" boomed Inspector Pines...

Levi Gravett (12)
Ysgol John Bright, Llandudno

Detective Marvin

My name's Detective Marvin. I'm in a muddle right now. I went to the local pub and got a little tipsy. Back at home, I popped on the TV and saw the convict I was looking for. I called the department, got the address and arrived. Worst mistake I ever made. I entered vision blurry, mind fogged up but this would be my only opportunity. Strolling along not sure where the eye-blinding convict was. I heard a footstep, it was the convict. With bad accuracy, I hit the chandelier ending him with one bullet, ending this wicked case for all.

Nosakhare Enaruna (12)
Ysgol John Bright, Llandudno

The Jewellery Shop Robbers

At midnight they broke in. They grabbed as many valuables as they could and put them in their bags. Mike thought it was a good idea to break into the till. However, Mike knocked a vase off the shelf which alerted the police. Mike quickly put the vase on the shelf and continued robbing the till. Suddenly, they heard sirens! Mike and his friends heard the sirens and tried to escape but it was too late... The police were waiting for them. The police called for backup. Once the backup arrived Mike realised one of the officers was his mum.

Maisie Brown (12)
Ysgol John Bright, Llandudno

Shadow Of A Murderer

I was standing at the broken building where the terrible crime happened. The only thing left was the dark brown door. I froze as a shadow appeared on the door. I started feeling a chill as I was the only one here. I walked towards the tall lonely door and touched the handle. I turned it slowly. As I opened the door someone was standing there. It was the person who was murdered. I stopped and thought about it. None of it made sense.

Julia Lament (12)
Ysgol John Bright, Llandudno

YOUNG WRITERS INFORMATION

We hope you have enjoyed reading this book – and that you will continue to in the coming years.

If you're the parent or family member of an enthusiastic poet or story writer, do visit our website **www.youngwriters.co.uk/subscribe** and sign up to receive news, competitions, writing challenges and tips, activities and much, much more! There's lots to keep budding writers motivated!

If you would like to order further copies of this book, or any of our other titles, then please give us a call or order via your online account.

Young Writers
Remus House
Coltsfoot Drive
Peterborough
PE2 9BF
(01733) 890066
info@youngwriters.co.uk

Join in the conversation!
Tips, news, giveaways and much more!

Join in the conversation!
Tips, news, giveaways and much more!

 YoungWritersUK @YoungWritersCW YoungWritersCW

Scan me to watch
the Unsolved video!